WWW.PLANTLOVEGROW.COM
WWW.DRSTEPHANIEMARGOLESE.COM

Photo of Elaheh Bos: credit Sabine YimLim

ISBN: 9781797482637

NOTE TO PARENTS AND TEACHERS:

As a parent, I know how important it is to find the answers that can help guide your child and give them the tools they need. This book was written from a desire to help children and their families, as well as those in their environment, understand the challenges and realities of ADHD.
I have met many wonderful "Billys" through my personal and professional life and found that they were often misunderstood because all people could focus on were the behavioural problems that followed them everywhere.
I hope that the children who relate to Billy's struggles will also be able to see themselves for all the amazing qualities that they have. This book aims to provide answers, encouragement, and give courage and hope in knowing that they have options and tools at their disposal. Dr. Margolese's guidance in sharing her experience and knowledge about ADHD was crucial in helping create a book that is more complete and offers a more balanced approach to the realities and challenges faced. Whatever choices you make to help your child through this journey, we wish you well.

Elaheh Bos

As a clinical child psychologist, I have had the opportunity to meet, evaluate, and develop treatment plans for numerous children who are struggling with ADHD. It is true that ADHD can look very different from one child to the next. Some children are primarily inattentive whereas others are more hyperactive and impulsive, and still others are inattentive, hyperactive, and impulsive. And because of how ADHD symptoms interfere with school life, a number of children with ADHD also have learning disabilities and/or emotional problems, such as anxiety. This means that each child who has ADHD has his or her own particular needs to consider.
From my perspective, you should arrange for a comprehensive psychological assessment to better understand the issues. Once you know what the diagnosis is, it becomes easier to figure out what is the best plan for your child. Certainly, there are different treatment options for managing ADHD. For many, it can be important to consider stimulant medication. I have seen how the medication helps these children function much better in the classroom, with friends, and within the family. That said, there are also other approaches and tools worth implementing that are the main focus of this book. We hope that you see this book as a helpful therapeutic resource for any child with ADHD.

Best wishes,
Dr. Stephanie

Billy Can't Slow Down!

By Elaheh Bos &
Stephanie Margolese, Ph.D.

BILLY THE RABBIT WAS GREAT AT WHAT HE LOVED TO DO. HE COULD PLAY FOR HOURS ON HIS FAVOURITE VIDEO GAME, RACING CARS AROUND ON NEVER-ENDING ROADS. BUT ANY TIME HE HAD TO DO SOMETHING THAT WAS LONG, DIFFICULT, OR A LITTLE BORING, IT BECAME VERY HARD FOR HIM. HE HAD TROUBLE PAYING ATTENTION AND CONCENTRATING, ESPECIALLY AT SCHOOL.

HE HAD ONLY ONE FRIEND BECAUSE THE OTHERS SAID HE WAS TOO PUSHY, AND INTERRUPTED TOO MUCH. HE SOMETIMES GOT INTO FIGHTS FOR SHOUTING WHATEVER CAME TO HIS MIND WITHOUT THINKING FIRST.
EVEN THOUGH BILLY LOVED PLAYING SOCCER IN THE SCHOOL TEAM AND TRIED TO DO HIS BEST IN CLASS, SCHOOL WAS NOT A VERY HAPPY PLACE FOR HIM.

AT HOME IT WASN'T SO EASY FOR HIM EITHER. BILLY ALWAYS SEEMED TO BE GETTING INTO TROUBLE, EVEN WHEN HE DIDN'T MEAN TO. HE COULDN'T KEEP HIS ROOM CLEAN, WAS ALWAYS LOSING HIS BELONGINGS, COULDN'T SIT FOR MORE THAN TWO MINUTES AT THE DINNER TABLE, AND WASN'T GOOD AT LISTENING TO HIS PARENTS UNTIL THE FIFTH TIME THEY ASKED HIM TO DO SOMETHING. SIMPLE TASKS LIKE MAKING HIS BED AND PUTTING OUT THE RECYCLING SEEMED IMPOSSIBLE TO REMEMBER, NO MATTER HOW HARD HE TRIED.

HIS TEACHER MISS ANNIE OFTEN REMINDED BILLY THAT HE COULD BE GREAT AT MANY THINGS...

IF HE ONLY SAT STILL LONG ENOUGH TO LISTEN, IF HE ONLY RAISED HIS HAND AND WAITED TO BE CALLED ON BEFORE BLURTING OUT THE ANSWER, AND IF HE ONLY FOCUSED A LITTLE MORE SO HE COULD FINISH HIS WORK.

MR. RUPERT WROTE NOTES DAILY TO HIS PARENTS ABOUT BILLY'S SHORT ATTENTION SPAN, INCOMPLETE HOMEWORK, AND ALL THE CARELESS MISTAKES HE MADE IN MATH CLASS.

MISS LEILA KEPT REPEATING THAT HE SHOULD SIT IN HIS SEAT AND NOT TALK OUT OF TURN.

Billy appeared to be in constant motion, moving about all the time. It was as if he had swallowed a whole bag of jumping beans that were making him bounce all through the day.

While Billy was smart, and kind, and tried really hard to listen, he couldn't seem to help himself from getting into all kinds of trouble.

"STOP JUMPING AROUND AND SLOW DOWN," HIS MOTHER WOULD SAY WHILE HE SPED THROUGH THE HOUSE EXPLAINING HIS DAY, A SANDWICH IN ONE HAND, A BALL IN THE OTHER, AND HIS HALF OPEN BACKPACK DRAGGING BEHIND HIM.

"YOU SHOULDN'T DO THAT," THE KIDS AT SCHOOL WOULD SHOUT AS BILLY JUMPED INTO MRS. HEDGEHOG'S THORN BUSH WITH HIS EYES CLOSED WHILE HOPPING ON ONE FOOT, BEFORE REALIZING IT WAS NOT A VERY GOOD IDEA.

Billy felt frustrated. Nobody seemed to understand him or see how hard he was trying to be the best rabbit he could be. He truly wanted to do better but simply couldn't. Words like inattentive, hyperactive, and impulsive followed him around everywhere he went.

Inattentive:
Not paying attention. Easily distracted. Daydreaming.

Hyperactive:
Extremely active. Constantly in motion. Always moving.

Impulsive:
Acting, doing or talking without thinking first. Quick to react.

WHEN MISS ANNIE SUGGESTED THEY GO SEE A DOCTOR WHO COULD TEST BILLY AND FIGURE OUT WHY HE IS STRUGGLING IN CLASS, HE DIDN'T KNOW HOW TO FEEL. BILLY ALWAYS FELT DIFFERENT FROM THE OTHERS AT SCHOOL, AS IF HE DIDN'T QUITE FIT IN. PART OF HIM WAS WORRIED THE DOCTOR WOULD FIND SOMETHING WRONG WITH HIM.

HE WAS ALSO A LITTLE CONFUSED BECAUSE HE WONDERED WHY HE NEEDED TO SEE A DOCTOR WHEN HE WASN'T HURT AND HE DIDN'T FEEL SICK.

BUT SECRETLY, DEEP DOWN INSIDE OF HIM, BILLY WAS HOPEFUL THAT THIS DOCTOR COULD HELP HIM.

Your Appointment
Name: Billy
Date: Sept. 14 Time: 2:30 PM
BE WELL MEDICAL CLINIC - 143 COURAGE STREET

APPOINTMENT
Name: Billy
Date: Oct. 12 Time: 10 AM
Dr. Melanie
Child and Family Psychologist
876 Compassion Road - office 45

Billy went to see:

His paediatrician:
A medical doctor specializing in children.

A child psychologist:
A doctor for children's feelings, thoughts, and behaviours who also does special testing.

HOPE?

JUICE

APPOINTMENT
Dr. Melanie
Child and Family Psychologist
Name: Billy
Date: Oct 12 Time: 10 AM

DR. MELANIE, THE PSYCHOLOGIST, ASKED A LOT OF QUESTIONS TO BILLY, HIS PARENTS AND ALSO SENT THEM BACK WITH QUESTIONS FOR HIS TEACHERS. SHE MET WITH BILLY ALONE A FEW TIMES AND HAD HIM DO DIFFERENT KINDS OF TESTS.*
AFTER PUTTING ALL THE RESULTS TOGETHER, SHE EXPLAINED THAT IT WAS **NOT** BILLY'S FAULT THAT HE IS HAVING TROUBLE PAYING ATTENTION. IT WAS **NOT** HIS FAULT THAT HE IS HYPERACTIVE AND IMPULSIVE. DR. MELANIE HELPED BILLY UNDERSTAND THAT HE HAS BEEN HAVING THESE CHALLENGES BECAUSE HIS BRAIN IS WIRED DIFFERENTLY.

***Psychological testing** for ADHD generally involves assessing cognitive skills (how you think and problem-solve verbally and visually, how efficiently you can process information, how well you remember and recall information) as well as attention skills (how well you maintain your attention over time, switch your attention from one task to another, and selectively attend to details while ignoring distractors). There are also other types of tests (e.g., academic achievement, visual-motor, socio-emotional) that could be administered depending on the needs of the child.

IT WAS WHILE SITTING IN AN OVERSIZED GREEN CHAIR WITH HIS FEET DANGLING OVER THE SIDE THAT BILLY LEARNED THAT HE HAD SOMETHING CALLED **ADHD**, AND THAT A LOT OF OTHER KIDS HAVE THIS SAME PROBLEM TOO.

"YOU ARE A SMART, CAPABLE, AND KIND LITTLE RABBIT," DR. MELANIE HAD SAID. "NOW THAT WE KNOW YOU HAVE **ADHD**, WE WILL WORK TOGETHER AS A TEAM WITH YOUR PARENTS AND TEACHERS TO MAKE SURE WE USE THE STRATEGIES AND TOOLS THAT WILL HELP YOU SUCCEED. VERY SOON, EVERYONE WILL SEE HOW AMAZING YOU ARE."

ADHD: Attention Deficit Hyperactivity Disorder
ADHD is a common behavioural disorder in which children have trouble paying attention and focusing, act without thinking (i.e., are impulsive) and are overly active or hyperactive. ADHD can affect children's abilities to function socially, academically, and at home. Children with ADHD may know what is expected of them but are unable to follow through because they can't sit still, focus on details, and sustain their attention nor can they help themselves from "acting out" or being disruptive.

BILLY FELT HOPEFUL AND AGREED TO KEEP AN OPEN MIND AS HIS PARENTS BROUGHT HIM TO DR. MELANIE AND HIS PAEDIATRICIAN A FEW MORE TIMES.

HE FELT EXCITED AND A LITTLE NERVOUS AS HE LOOKED AT THE CLOUDS OUTSIDE THE WINDOW ON THE TRAIN RIDE HOME. THERE WERE A LOT OF DIFFERENT OPTIONS AND STRATEGIES TO TRY BUT HE WAS READY TO HELP FIGURE OUT WHAT THE BEST PLAN WAS FOR HIM.

There are different treatments and approaches for managing ADHD, which should be tailored to the particular needs of your child. These can include:

Medication: A trial of stimulant medication prescribed by your family doctor, paediatrician or a child psychiatrist.

An Individualized Education Plan (IEP) with accommodations at school: Having more time to complete work; modifying the workload; using fidget toys or special cushions; sitting at the front of the class; improving organization of work; breaking down tasks into smaller steps; taking frequent breaks.

Changing the structure and environment at home: Maintaining a regular schedule and morning and bedtime routines; increasing physical activity; adopting healthier eating habits; improving organization of workspace and belongings; developing communication and problem-solving skills.

Positive reinforcement: Praising and recognizing efforts to improve behaviour; "catching" and rewarding desirable behaviours.

AT SCHOOL, BILLY AND HIS TEACHERS CAME UP WITH A PLAN AND MADE SOME CHANGES BASED ON DR. MELANIE'S ADVICE, SO THAT THINGS WOULD BE EASIER FOR HIM.

BILLY NOW SAT IN FRONT OF THE CLASS AND CLOSER TO HIS TEACHER TO HELP HIM PAY MORE ATTENTION TO THE LESSONS.

WHENEVER HE FELT LIKE HE NEEDED TO MOVE AND JUMP, HE SIGNALLED MISS ANNIE AND WAS ALLOWED TO HOP AROUND THE HALLS FOR A FEW MINUTES BEFORE COMING BACK TO HIS SEAT.

School

TO KEEP TRACK OF SCHOOL ASSIGNMENTS, HE STARTED TO USE A CALENDAR AND REMINDER NOTES. WITH MISS ANNIE, HE WOULD REVIEW THE LIST OF THE WORK TO DO IN ORDER OF WHAT WAS MOST IMPORTANT TO MAKE SURE NOTHING WAS FORGOTTEN.

MR. RUPERT ALLOWED HIM TO HAVE EXTRA TIME TO FINISH HIS TESTS AND HIS WORK, WHICH HELPED HIM DO BETTER IN SCHOOL.

WITH SOME PRACTICE, BILLY LEARNED TO COUNT TO FIVE IN HIS HEAD AND RAISE HIS HAND BEFORE ANSWERING. HE NOTICED HE WAS GETTING A LOT MORE PRAISE FOR TALKING ONLY WHEN IT WAS HIS TURN.

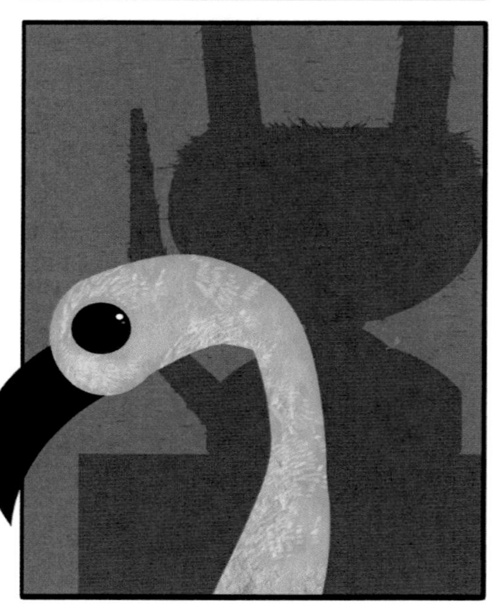

HE LEARNED TO BREAK BIG PROJECTS INTO SMALLER STEPS AND HE STARTED TO WORK IN SHORTER BLOCKS OF TIME. BILLY WAS ALLOWED TO TAKE 2 TO 5 MINUTES TO STRETCH, HOP AROUND, DRINK WATER, HAND OUT PAPERS, OR EVEN DRAW AFTER EACH SECTION OF SCHOOLWORK WAS COMPLETED. HE FOUND THIS HELPED HIM TO CONCENTRATE BETTER.

BILLY AND HIS TEACHERS USED COLOURS TO ORGANIZE HIS SCHOOLWORK.

TO HELP HIM BE LESS IMPULSIVE IN CLASS, MISS LEILA CREATED VISUAL SIGNALS FOR INTERRUPTIONS. IT WAS KIND OF A SPECIAL SECRET CODE TO REMIND BILLY TO WAIT FOR HIS TURN.

HE ESPECIALLY LIKED BEING ABLE TO SQUEEZE HIS NEW STRESS BALL IN CLASS TO KEEP HIS PAWS BUSY WHEN HE WAS FEELING RESTLESS.

THINGS THAT USED TO FEEL OVERWHELMING AND COMPLICATED BECAME MUCH EASIER AND EVEN ENJOYABLE.

AT HOME, AND WITH HIS PARENTS' HELP, BILLY'S ROOM WAS RE-ORGANIZED TO MAKE IT TIDY. EVERYTHING HAD A PLACE, CATEGORY, AND LABEL SO THAT HE COULD GET READY QUICKLY IN THE MORNING AND MORE EASILY FIND WHAT HE NEEDED. HIS SCHOOL BAG WAS PREPARED AT NIGHT FOR THE NEXT DAY SO THAT HE NO LONGER HANDED IN UNFINISHED ASSIGNMENTS THAT SMELLED LIKE PEANUT BUTTER SANDWICHES.

THEY ALSO CREATED A SYSTEM TO KEEP CLUTTER AT BAY. EVEN THOUGH HE DIDN'T WANT TO ADMIT IT, BILLY LOVED HIS NEW ORGANIZED HOMEWORK STATION.

BILLY AND HIS PARENTS ALSO MADE OTHER KINDS OF CHANGES. AFTER SCHOOL AND EATING A SNACK, BILLY NOW HAD FREE TIME TO JUMP AND ROLL AROUND IN THE FIELD OR PLAY SOCCER WITH THE NEIGHBOURS. HE LIKED THESE ACTIVITIES BECAUSE HE FELT CALMER WHEN IT WAS TIME TO DO HIS HOMEWORK.

WITH THE NEW SYSTEMS THAT HIS PARENTS DEVELOPED, HE SAW THE ORDER OF CERTAIN ACTIVITIES AND ROUTINES AND HAD VISUAL REMINDERS OF THE STEPS THAT HE NEEDED TO FINISH BEFORE STARTING SOMETHING NEW.

BILLY AND HIS PARENTS LOOKED AT HIS EATING HABITS TO SEE IF SOME HEALTHIER FOOD CHOICES COULD HELP WITH HIS EXCESS ENERGY AND IMPROVE HIS FOCUS.

BILLY'S NIGHTLY SCHEDULE AND ROUTINE WERE CHANGED SO THAT IT WAS THE SAME EVERY NIGHT AND HE COULD WIND DOWN AND RELAX SOONER. THIS HELPED HIM TO REST PROPERLY AND EVEN GET MORE SLEEP.

THEY ALSO WORKED ON TALKING TOGETHER MORE REGULARLY ABOUT PROBLEMS THAT CAME UP AT HOME, AT SCHOOL, OR WITH FRIENDS. BILLY AND HIS PARENTS PRACTICED HOW TO PROBLEM-SOLVE. THESE TOOLS HELPED UN-SHUFFLE ALL THE INFORMATION IN HIS BRAIN AND KEEP HIM FOCUSED ON EACH TASK AT HAND.

How to problem-solve:

1. Identify the problem.

2. List all possible solutions (including the pros and cons of each idea).

3. Choose the one that seems best.

4. Try it out and see if it worked.

5. If it didn't work, choose another idea.

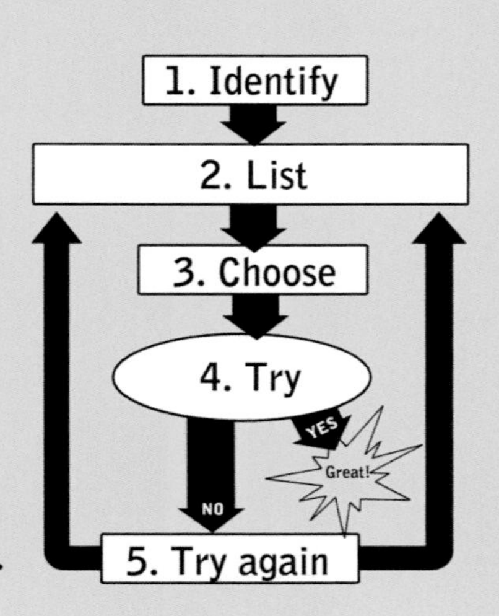

As time passed and Billy became familiar with all these new tools, he became really good at understanding, planning, checking his calendar, putting things in order, and making lists.

HE STILL VISITED DR. MELANIE ONCE IN A WHILE, BUT IT WAS MOSTLY TO TELL HER HOW GREAT THINGS WERE GOING.

SOMETIMES THEY PRACTICED NEW WAYS OF HOLDING A THOUGHT SO THAT BILLY COULD BE IN CONTROL OF THE WORDS COMING OUT. HE WAS GRATEFUL THAT SHE UNDERSTOOD HIM AND WAS THERE TO HELP.

BILLY FELT PROUD OF HIMSELF FOR ALL HE HAD ACCOMPLISHED WITH HIS FAMILY, DOCTORS, AND TEACHERS. SOME OF THE STUDENTS AT SCHOOL UNDERSTOOD HIM BETTER TOO AND HE MADE NEW FRIENDS HE COULD INVITE OVER AND PLAY VIDEO GAMES WITH.

AND WHEN A NEW STUDENT CAME AND BILLY SAW ALL THE OLD SIGNS OF WHAT HE HAD GONE THROUGH, BILLY KNEW THAT HE COULD BE BRAVE, SHARE HIS STORY, AND HELP SOMEONE ELSE FIGURE OUT WHAT THE BEST PLAN IS FOR THEM.

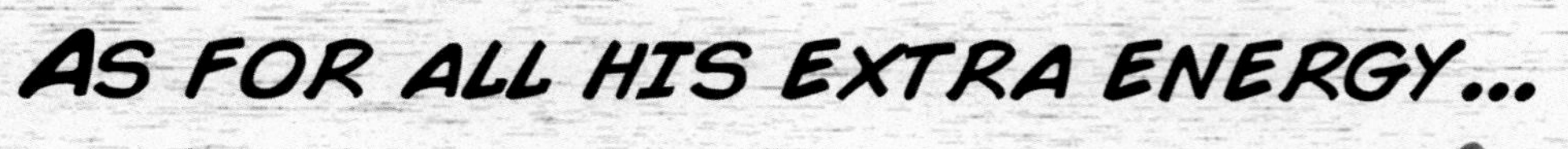
AS FOR ALL HIS EXTRA ENERGY...

BILLY AND HIS NEW
FRIENDS KNEW
EXACTLY WHAT
TO DO WITH THAT.
Join the team!
Tryouts
Tuesday afternoon!
3:00 PM
8
CAPTAIN

Summary of Strategies To Manage ADHD

by Stephanie Margolese, Ph.D.

It's not easy to be different and to struggle with paying attention, listening to adults, sitting still, and completing all of your chores and work. The good news is that there are things you can do, just like Billy, to make your everyday life better and easier for you.
Try these strategies and tools to see what works best for you.

School:
Strategies To Manage Inattention

- Sit in front of the class and closer to the teacher to help with attention issues.
- Arrange to have extra time to finish tests and work because it generally takes longer for you to complete the work.
- Learn to break big projects into smaller steps so that the work is manageable and less overwhelming.
- Work in 15-20 minute blocks of time. After each section of work is completed, take a short break to stretch, walk around, drink water, hand out papers, or draw.
- Use a calendar and reminder notes to keep track of your school assignments. Find someone to help you review the list of the work to do in order of what is most important and to make sure nothing is forgotten.
- Use different colours to organize your work and for each class subject.
- Have a system to let your teacher know how you are doing (e.g., stuck, struggling, got it or red, yellow, green).

Strategies To Manage Hyperactivity/Impulsivity

- If you need to move around, have a signal with your teacher that permits you to stand up and stretch or leave the classroom and walk around the halls for a few minutes. Have another visual signal to remind you to wait your turn.
- Practice counting to five in your head and raising your hand before blurting out an answer in class.
- Squeeze a stress ball or play with a fidget toy in class to keep your hands busy.

HOME:
STRATEGIES TO MANAGE INATTENTION

- Keep your room tidy. Every thing should have its own place, category, and label so that you can more easily find what you need. When you take something out, put it back as soon as you are done with it.
- Prepare your school bag and clothes at night. This way you will be ready to leave quickly in the morning and you won't forget your homework.
- Have an organized and neat homework station to do your work and minimize distractions.
- After 15-20 minutes of doing homework, take a short break to move around and get a drink of water. Set a limit as to how much homework you have to do each day.
- Keep an agenda, calendar, and schedule to know and plan for what is coming up.
- Prepare checklists of what you need to do and make visual reminders of the tasks you need to finish before starting something new. For fun, create reminder songs like '1,2,3 do I have everything with me? Check!'

STRATEGIES TO MANAGE HYPERACTIVITY/IMPULSIVITY

- After school, make sure to have a snack and free time to run around, shoot some hoops, or play a sport to get rid of extra energy before trying to sit down to do your homework.
- Try to keep the same schedule and routine every night so that you can wind down and relax sooner, get more rest, and enough sleep.
- Take a look at your eating habits to see if some healthier food choices could help with your excess energy and improve your focus.
- Try a special cushion that challenges your balance on your chair to help you stay seated longer at the dinner table.

Practice talking with your parents regularly.
Share about your concerns or problems that happen at home, school, or with friends. Learn to communicate and problem-solve issues.

Just like Billy, you can feel proud for making the changes that allow you to manage your ADHD and for knowing you have found the plan that works best for you. Keep it up!

Elaheh Bos is the founder of Plant Love Grow, a resource site that creates tools to help parents, teachers and health professionals.

She is a passionate public speaker, an artist, illustrator, author and entrepreneur who believes in our innate capacity to bloom.

She loves to write books, create new journals and collaborate on different projects with amazing people.

Download free printable pages:

www.plantlovegrow.com/Billy

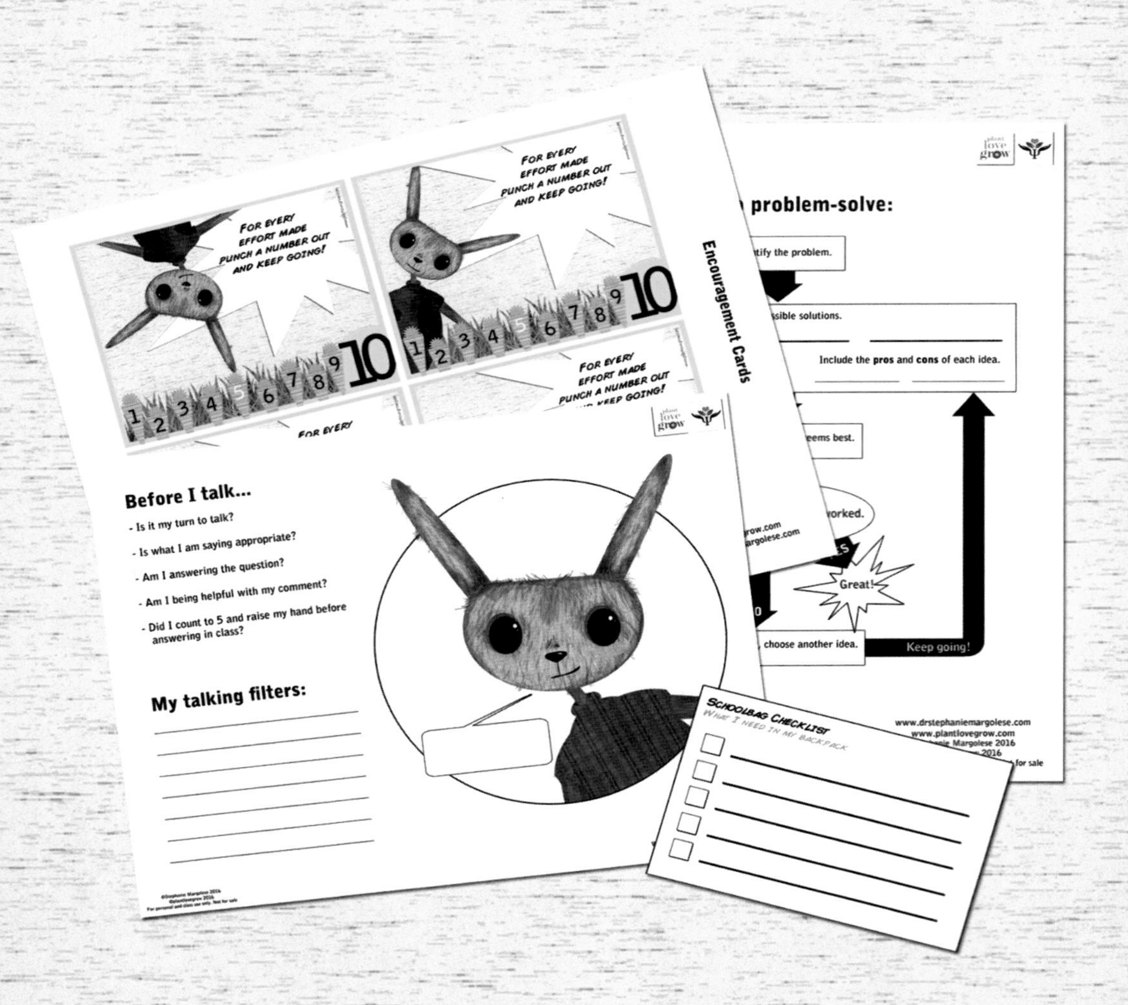

Dr. Stephanie Margolese is a clinical psychologist who specializes in assessing and treating children, adolescents, and their families. She has worked in the Child Psychiatry Outpatient Department at the Jewish General Hospital since 2001.

Dr. Margolese is an Assistant Professor (Joint) (Professional) in the Department of Psychology, Faculty of Science and in the Department of Psychiatry, Faculty of Medicine at McGill University.

In addition to her mission to help children reach their full potential, she has discovered a passion for writing and collaborating on therapeutic resource books for children.

For more information about ADHD:

www.drstephaniemargolese.com/Billy

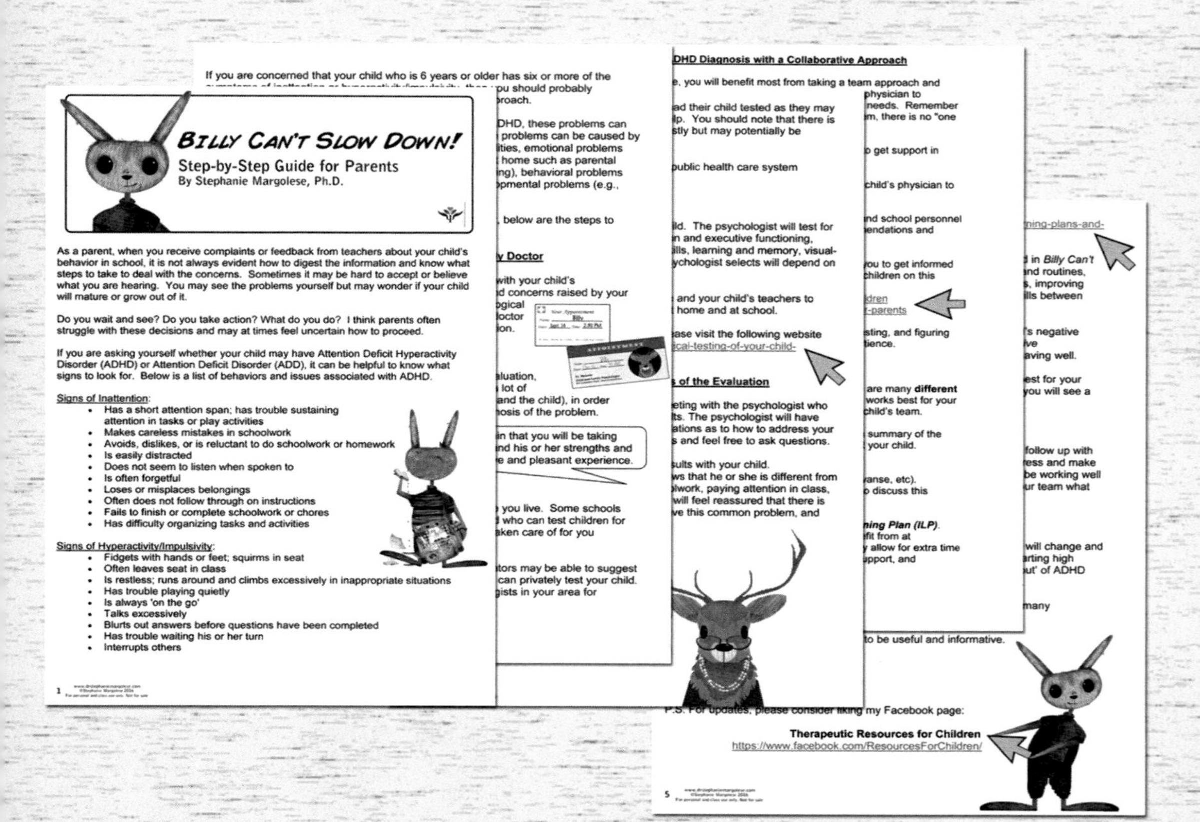

BILLY CAN'T SLOW DOWN!

Step-by-Step Guide for Parents

By Stephanie Margolese, Ph.D.

As a parent, when you receive complaints or feedback from teachers about your child's behavior in school, it is not always evident how to digest the information and know what steps to take to deal with the concerns. Sometimes it may be hard to accept or believe what you are hearing. You may see the problems yourself but may wonder if your child will mature or grow out of it.

Do you wait and see? Do you take action? What do you do? I think parents often struggle with these decisions and may at times feel uncertain how to proceed.

If you are asking yourself whether your child may have Attention Deficit Hyperactivity Disorder (ADHD) or Attention Deficit Disorder (ADD), it can be helpful to know what signs to look for. Below is a list of behaviors and issues associated with ADHD.

Signs of Inattention:

- Has a short attention span; has trouble sustaining attention in tasks or play activities
- Makes careless mistakes in schoolwork
- Avoids, dislikes, or is reluctant to do schoolwork or homework
- Is easily distracted
- Does not seem to listen when spoken to
- Is often forgetful
- Loses or misplaces belongings
- Often does not follow through on instructions
- Fails to finish or complete schoolwork or chores
- Has difficulty organizing tasks and activities

Signs of Hyperactivity/Impulsivity:

- Fidgets with hands or feet; squirms in seat
- Often leaves seat in class
- Is restless; runs around and climbs excessively in inappropriate situations
- Has trouble playing quietly
- Is always 'on the go'
- Talks excessively
- Blurts out answers before questions have been completed
- Has trouble waiting his or her turn
- Interrupts others

P.S. For updates, please consider liking my Facebook page:

Therapeutic Resources for Children

https://www.facebook.com/ResourcesForChildren/

How to stop focusing on worries

Anger management

Coping with sadness

Coping with fear and phobias

Other collaborations by these authors

WWW.PLANTLOVEGROW.COM
WWW.DRSTEPHANIEMARGOLESE.COM

Made in the USA
Monee, IL
06 June 2021